Joe's Story

by

Rachel Anderson

Illustrated by Nick Ward

First published in Great Britain by Barrington Stoke Ltd
10 Belford Terrace, Edinburgh EH4 3DQ
Copyright © 2001 Rachel Anderson
Illustrations © Nick Ward
The moral right of the author has been asserted in
accordance with the Copyright, Designs and
Patents Act 1988
ISBN 1-902260-70-8
Printed by Polestar AUP Aberdeen Ltd

A Note from the Author

Once, a while ago, I knew a boy whose Mum died and whose Dad was in prison. The boy had a grandmother. But she refused to have anything to do with him. So he was taken to live in a Children's Home. He grew up without a family to care for him. He was always lonely.

Remembering that boy gave me the starting point for writing *Joe's Story*. But I wanted to see if I could work out a more hopeful future.

To Ellen Wharam,
champion reader

Contents

Chapter 1
Grandad and Me

My Grandad and I had always lived together. Just the two of us. We had a flat on the Highfield Estate.

Grandad's name was Joe, same as me.

"You know," he'd say when I was small, "we're very alike. It's a wonder people can tell us apart."

That was one of Grandad's little jokes. Of course people could tell us apart. He was an old man with a grey beard and I was just a small boy then.

Not many boys lived alone with their grandad. Most of lived with their mum or their dad and sometimes both. They had aunties and grandmothers, big brothers and little brothers, sisters and cousins. For me, there was never anybody else to take care of me except Grandad.

Every day when I came out of school, he would be waiting for me.

One night as I was getting ready for bed, I told Grandad about the boy I sat next to at school. "His mum's just had a new baby," I said. "He told us in Class News."

"Ah. That'll be nice for him, won't it?" Grandad said as he tucked me up and kissed the top of my head. "Goodnight then, Joe. God bless." He didn't even ask whether it was a boy or a girl.

"Grandad," I said, "our family's not the same as other people's, is it?"

"Course not, Joe," said Grandad. "Every family is different. Every single family in the world."

"But why is ours so small?" I asked him. I didn't mind. After all, Grandad and I got on well.

Grandad said, "Because small is beautiful."

I didn't ask any more questions. I felt
there were things Grandad didn't like to
talk about. For instance, I knew I'd once had
a Grandma. There was a photo of her by
Grandad's bed. It wasn't in colour, just
black and white. But he didn't talk about
her.

Then, just before my seventh birthday, something interesting happened that changed our family.

Grandad met me, same as usual, outside school. But we didn't go home right away. "This way, Joe," he said.

"Where to?" I said.

"We're going to meet someone. A new friend. To see if we like her."

What did he mean? I didn't realise our family was about to get bigger. We walked for ages, way over to the other side of the Highfield Estate. My legs were aching. I was only young then.

Grandad said, "Not far now. You see, Joe, I met this chap in the Post Office the other day. He told me about his bitch. Her name is Sweetheart."

I thought Grandad was talking rude talk. But he explained that 'bitch' was the word for a female dog.

"She's half labrador, half something else. A mongrel in fact, but ever so good-looking and she's just had puppies."

When we reached the house, the dog's owner took us down the garden to his shed. We saw the female dog lying on a blanket with her four puppies sleeping round her. You could see why they called her Sweetheart. She was a lovely golden colour.

The owner's wife had already named the puppies. "Honey, Popsicle, Sugar and Darling," she said proudly.

I said, "But these puppies are all blind!" Their eyes were sealed shut.

"Puppies are always like that when they're newborn," Grandad said. "But give them a few weeks and their eyes will be opening and they'll be all over the place."

Grandad chose Honey to be ours. On the way home, he said, "We can always change the name when she comes to us."

"Oh no," I said. "I like it."

When Honey was eight weeks, we went back to fetch her and bring her home. We

bought a rug for her to sleep on as well as a new collar and lead.

Grandad said, "So now our family's just the right size, isn't it?"

So there we were, the three of us, Grandad, Honey and me, getting along happily together.

Even though we lived in a small flat and we didn't have a garden or a shed, Grandad made sure Honey was properly cared for. He said that she belonged to both of us. But really she was his. Wherever he went, Honey went too. She kept him company while I was at school. She kept him healthy too. They took good walks every day.

One evening, Grandad and Honey had just come in from their walk, when someone knocked at our front door.

Chapter 2
Bad Lad

Grandad had gone to put the kettle on. I was doing my homework in the living room. So I went to answer the door. A man in a smart suit was standing there.

"Hi there," he said grinning, but not at me.

Honey padded over and twitched her ears.

"Got a dog now I see," the man said. "Here boy, good boy."

I was about to tell him that Honey wasn't a male but a female when the man pushed his way past me.

"The old fellow home, is he?" the visitor asked and made straight for the kitchen as if he knew the flat. He said something to Grandad and I saw Grandad give him something. I think it was money.

"Would you like a cup of tea?" I asked him.

But the man went out again as fast as

he'd come in. I made the tea anyway because Grandad looked so upset.

"I suppose you know who that was?" he said.

"Well yes," I said. "I sort of guessed." It was my Dad. I didn't really remember him. I wanted to ask Grandad how come my Dad didn't live with us. But I didn't like to. So instead I asked, "How old was my Dad when he had me?"

Grandad said, "Too young to have kids. He was always too young and he always will be. Even as a boy, he always looked for trouble. He got in with a bad crowd, even at school. He just couldn't keep away from the wrong sort. He would go missing too. Sometimes we'd not hear from him for months. When he got married, me and your Gran never even knew about it till later."

I said, "And my Mum, she wasn't a bad woman, was she?"

Grandad shook his head. "No, she was a sweet little thing. Not that we saw much of her. She'd have been the making of him if he'd bothered to stick with her."

I knew my Mum had died suddenly. She had a weak heart.

"A tragedy that was," Grandad said. "And you were only three. Your Dad tried to look after you for a bit but he wasn't any good at it. So the people from the social services said you'd have to be put in a Home."

At school, I knew two boys who lived in a Children's Home. They said it wasn't too bad. But that was because they had each other. But I knew I wouldn't have liked it.

"It was OK, Joe," Grandad said. "You never got put in care. Just in time, your Gran found out. And she wouldn't have it. 'I'm his Gran. I'll take care of him,' she said. She had to do it real quick before the social workers could get you. She used to say, she didn't kidnap you. She grand-kidnapped you."

Grandad began to smile as he remembered the past. "It was in all the newspapers, you know." He took some old newspaper cuttings from the drawer and showed me.

'GRANDMOTHER'S FIGHT FOR HER RIGHTS,' the headlines said. And 'VICTORY FOR BATTLING GRAN.'

"Gran wasn't to know she had so little time left herself. When she died, a nosy social worker was round here the next day to take you away."

"What did you do?" I asked him.

"I was all on my own and you were howling all the time. I have to say, I did think about letting them have you. But only for half a minute. I thought, poor kid! His Mum and his Gran are both dead. His Dad has gone walkabout and nobody knows when *he'll* turn up again. I thought, I'm all little Joe's got left. What's more, he's all I've got. So we'd better hang on to each other."

16

"Thanks, Grandad. I'm glad you *did* hang on to me. And I'm glad you've told me."

Grandad gave a deep sigh. "It's best you should know."

Part of me really wanted to see my Dad again even if he wasn't much good. But over the next five years, he only called in a couple of times and he never stopped long enough to chat.

So Grandad and I carried on as we were, with him growing older and me growing up.

****

"One of us is changing," Grandad said one day. "Either you're getting taller or I'm shrinking."

"Course you're not shrinking!" I said.

But he was. It's what happens to old people. I learnt that in Human Biology. His beard had turned white too and his hands trembled.

"Come over here, Joe, stand up against the wall and let's see how tall you are." He stood me behind the kitchen door where he'd been marking off my height ever since I was three. "Steady now. Feet flat on the floor. No cheating."

He took my Maths book off the table and held it level on my head. He took a pencil from my pencil case. He compared the last mark with this one.

"Yup," he said with satisfaction. "You've

grown two inches since Christmas. You'll soon be a man. Then it's down the mines with you to earn your living."

That was another of his jokes. There's no coal mines round here. Just factories and farming and not a lot of jobs to be had anyway.

But he didn't want me to go looking for a job. He wanted me to stay on at school, then go to College.

"You make something of yourself," he said. "Get yourself a better education than I ever had."

He'd never had the chance himself. That's why he wanted it so much for me. He'd left school at fourteen. There'd been a war on. Grandad often talked about what subjects I should study. He thought something to do with computers would be good. I said something about Design Technology.

He said, "Yes, that's good too. After all, it's your life. Whatever you choose, I'll back you. Though I can't say it won't be hard for me when you leave home. I'll probably shed a tear or two."

"No you won't, Grandad!" He was too tough to cry.

"Well, I'll be crying on the inside anyhow, until you come home in your vacations ..."

"My whats?"

"Vacations. That's what they call holidays at College. When you come home, I'll be taking you round the estate to show you off to the neighbours."

"Oh, no you won't, Grandad! Mrs Harrison will want to kiss me." She was our neighbour in the flat upstairs. She still treated me as though I was about six.

"And you'll deserve more than a kiss, Joe." Grandad always smiled to himself as he dreamed of my glorious future.

So that was the way we planned it. I'd work hard and get to go to College. He'd miss me. But he'd have Honey and Mrs Harrison to keep an eye on him. And he'd be pleased to see me back in the holidays.

We weren't to know it wouldn't turn out that way. And it was probably better that we didn't.

Chapter 3
Dad's Back

"Grandad, we've got Parents' Evening on Friday," I said.

It was the big one when we discussed our subjects for the next two years. "But you don't need to come." I knew he had been feeling tired lately.

"Course I'm coming! I'm your supporter's club. Do you want your teachers to think nobody cares?"

He put on a fresh shirt and a bright, flowery tie. He combed his beard and his hair. He looked very old-fashioned.

Some boys hanging around the bus stop cheered when we went past, but afterwards, I heard them laughing at us. I knew them. They'd left school last term. But they hadn't got jobs yet.

In the school hall, nobody's parents had dressed up as much as my Grandad. But I knew it showed how much he cared about me. And it would be much worse not to have anyone, like some kids.

There wasn't much to discuss with the teachers, of course. It was all decided. Grandad and I had already talked it through so many times. But I knew he liked hearing them praise me.

"Well done, Joe," he said afterwards. "All your teachers are pleased with you. You're working hard. Let's go for some chips and fizzy pop to celebrate."

"OK." Poor old Grandad. Fizzy pop went out with the ark. No-one would have known what he was talking about.

****

The very next morning my Dad turned up again.

"Hi, Dad!" he shouted to Grandad. It sounded funny hearing him call my Grandad 'Dad'. "I'm taking the boy out for the day. Let him see a bit of the world for a change."

I wasn't sure about leaving Grandad behind. Saturday was when I walked with him and Honey down by the canal. But he said, "Go on and enjoy yourself."

I went to find my trainers. My Dad yelled at me, "Hurry up or I'll go without you. I can't wait about all day."

At first it was great being with Dad. We kicked a ball about for a while. He was ace with his footwork, even wearing ordinary shoes. Then we went on a bus and met up in a pub with some of his pals. Dad made a speech.

"Today," he said, "it is my proud duty, as a father, to offer my son his first pint of beer."

"I'm only fourteen," I said.

"Shut up," he replied.

His friends cheered. I didn't much like the taste of the beer. Too watery.

"Got any more cash on you, son?" my Dad asked.

"What for?" I asked him.

He was patting my pockets before I had

time to say anything. He got my wallet. There was a tenner in it.

My Dad laughed. "Is that all you've got? Keeps you pretty short, doesn't he, the mean, old skinflint?" He was talking about Grandad.

"That's for next week's dinners," I protested.

Dad took the tenner anyway. "You'll get it back. It's only a loan." He laughed as he said it.

He didn't look me in the eye so I knew he was lying. But I didn't want to believe it. He bought another round of beers. I didn't want any more. So I went outside and sat on a bench. I wondered if Grandad and Honey were still down by the canal.

The afternoon dragged on. Dad came out and said, "We'll go for a curry in a while. OK?" then went back inside.

But he must have left soon after by another door.

I didn't see him again.

****

I found my own way home. I had to walk. I hadn't any money for the bus.

Honey was lying by the gas fire. The sausages were sizzling in the pan.

"Hello, Joe," said Grandad.

"Grandad – " I started to say.

"Eat your tea first," said Grandad. "We'll talk later."

But we didn't. There was nothing to say.

We watched telly instead, side by side on the settee. It was a thriller. It was a good evening. I went to bed really happy.

Chapter 4
Gone Missing

On Monday afternoon, there was a surprise waiting for me when I got home from school. And it wasn't a nice one.

The front door was locked. That was very odd. I could hear Honey whining inside. Luckily I had my own key and let myself in. Grandad wasn't there. Honey was on her own.

"Hello, girl," I said. "Where's Grandad gone then?"

She wagged her tail. She could tell me she was pleased to see me. But she couldn't tell me where her master was.

I began to get worried. So I went up to Mrs Harrison's flat.

"Yes, dear. They came for him about dinner time," she told me.

"Who did?"

"The ambulance men. Nice friendly chaps. They carried him out on a stretcher.

He did look poorly."

"Where did they take him?"

"To hospital, I'm afraid."

"Which one?"

"I think it was Saint Luke's, dear."

Grandad had taken me there once when I came off my skateboard in the park and broke my arm.

I slipped Honey's lead on and we set off at a fast jog. When we reached Saint Luke's Hospital, Honey wasn't allowed in.

"This isn't a zoo, my friend," said the woman at the reception desk. So I had to take Honey out and tie her up to a railing

near the porter's lodge. The porter said he'd keep an eye on her while I visited Grandad.

It took me ages to find his ward. When I did, the first thing he asked was, "Where's my Honey?"

"It's all right. She's downstairs. She's tied up by the porter's lodge."

"You're sure she'll not come to harm?"

"He's keeping an eye on her," I told him.

"She hasn't had her walkies today. Poor girl."

"Oh, but she's walked all the way here with me," I said.

I was thinking that they should have let her in. She'd have cheered him up. He was upset and angry about being in bed.

"They say I've got to stay here while they do some tests. Silly fools. I'm fit as a fiddle. That doctor! I'll bet he's no older than you."

The nurse wouldn't tell me anything. She thought I was too young. "We really need to speak with one of the adult members of his family in case there are papers to be signed."

"I'm his family. Anyway, what papers?" I asked.

But she wouldn't say.

"What about your Mum or Dad? Where are they?" she wanted to know.

I didn't talk to her about my Dad. It was too difficult. She wouldn't understand. "I haven't got a Dad or a Mum," I said.

Chapter 5
Visitors

When visiting time was over they rang a bell. It gave me a fright.

"Off you go now," the nurse said.

I didn't want to leave Grandad there on his own. I said, "Will you be all right?"

Funny thing was that *he* was worrying about *me* being on my own at home.

"How are you going to manage, Joe?"

"Grandad!" I said. "I'm nearly fifteen. I'm quite capable of looking after myself for a day or so. When you were my age, you were already out at work."

"You'll be needing some more money, Joe, to see you through the week."

He was right. I would. Even if I felt too worried to be hungry, nothing would stop Honey eating her dinner.

"You find my pension book, Joe. Bring it in tomorrow. I'll sign next week's order. You can cash it at the Post Office."

"OK. Goodnight, Grandad. Sleep well."

"You too." He gave me a hug.

"See you in the morning," I said.

"No you won't," said Grandad firmly. "In the morning, I'll be having a nice lie-in and you've got to go to school. You're not using me as an excuse to skive."

Grandad wasn't joking. He wanted me to do well in my exams.

****

So I went to school, same as usual. I had to set the alarm clock for earlier than usual to make sure I had enough time to give Honey a quick walk first. I thought of

43

asking Mrs Harrison to take Honey out at midday. But Mrs Harrison was a bit shaky on her legs. I thought Honey might pull her over. Then I'd have two oldies lying in hospital beds.

In the evening, Honey had a proper walk across town. She got a good welcome from the porter too.

But Grandad wasn't looking so good. He was cheerful but a bit yellow and very tired even though it was only half past four.

I'd brought him some things I thought he'd need – clean hankies, a newspaper, his spare glasses case, his photo of my Gran ('The grand-kidnapper') from beside his bed and a bar of milk chocolate I'd bought from the hospital shop down by the main entrance.

I got to know the area by the main entrance really well over the next few weeks. It was always busy with staff rushing this way and that, visitors coming and going, patients shuffling slowly.

"It's more like a railway station than a hospital," I told Grandad. "There's a coffee shop, a bookshop and a place you can buy a burger and chips. I won't starve even if you have to stay in all week."

And Grandad did have to stay in all week. And the next week too.

I kept half-hoping my Dad might turn up. Even if he didn't bring a big bunch of

flowers, he could at least say 'Hello' to his own Dad.

But he never did turn up.

One Friday evening, as I was getting Honey back from the porter's lodge, a woman came up to me and told me that her name was Miss Pope and that she was a social worker. She'd been sent to talk to me.

I was quite surprised. I asked her why I needed a social worker.

She said, "I've only just heard how you're living on your own. I'll need to come and visit you at home. See how you're coping."

That really annoyed me. I was coping fine. It was Grandad everyone needed to worry about.

I said, "I'm not really on my own. There's Mrs Harrison upstairs. I can ask her if I need anything."

Not that I would.

Miss Pope smiled. "Yes, I know. But I still have to do my visit. How about tomorrow? D'you get up early or late on Saturdays?"

"Depends," I said. Then, "Oh, all right." She had a job to do. The quicker she did it, the sooner she'd be off my back.

"Any time," I told her.

"Fine. Say, between eight thirty and nine tomorrow morning?"

On my way home, I changed my mind. I decided that tomorrow I'd get up extra early. I'd be out on a long walk with Honey when that nosy Miss Pope called.

****

I was nearly home when I heard two voices. They called to me from out of the shadows just beside our block of flats.

"Hi, Joe!" said one.

"Hello there!" said the other.

It was Dean and Matt from school. They came over to me.

"Your old man, still away is he?" Matt asked.

How did they know that? But it was nice of them to ask.

"Yup. They're keeping him in for tests," I told them.

"Still got the place to yourself, then?" said Matt.

"Bet you're having a great time!" said Dean.

"Not really," I said.

Being on my own in that small flat, night after night, was getting me down. I'd even been letting Honey sleep on my bed. She wasn't supposed to come into the bedrooms. But some nights when I got really depressed, I needed to hear her breathing. It made me feel safer.

Matt said, "Want some male company?"

"OK," I said. "I'll make some tea."

Then two more boys I didn't know came tagging along behind Matt and Dean. They had plastic bags clinking with cans.

Matt said, "Hi! You coming over to Joe's place too?"

"No, Matt," I said. "I said just you and Dean. For a quick cup of tea. That's all."

"Cup of tea?" Matt laughed. "You're joking!"

Dean said, "Your old Grandad won't mind."

Matt and Dean quickly made themselves at home in Grandad's flat.

"Where's the music?"

They found Grandad's radio on the chair by his bed.

Just then there was a knock at the door. It was more visitors arriving. I didn't even know them.

"Please, Matt," I begged. "Don't let them in. Tell them to go somewhere else."

But it was too late. Word was spreading.

Matt saw Honey lying under the table. After a few beers, he began to show off.

He took a rasher of bacon from the fridge and held it over Honey's nose. He tried to make her jump for it.

"Look at me!" said Matt. "Dog training!"

If Honey decided to give him a warning nip, things could turn nasty.

"Don't tease her!" I shouted.

The front room was crammed with people. "Please try and keep the noise down," I begged.

"Come on, Joe," said Dean smiling. "Relax. We're only having fun."

He was right. I might as well enjoy the party. I took the can he held out to me and tugged at the ring pull. Fizz went the beer. I sipped. I drank. It was cold and I liked it. I stopped worrying.

The next thing I remember was waking up at three a.m. They'd all gone. The front room looked terrible. It smelled of beer and cigarette smoke.

I stumbled off to bed and shut my eyes. I'd clear up in the morning. Thank goodness Grandad wasn't here.

Suddenly, I was sitting up again. No way could I sleep now – Miss Pope – she was coming to visit first thing. To see how I was coping. Any time after eight thirty. She must not see this mess. Whatever happened, I had to clear it up before her visit.

Or I'd be in deep water.

Chapter 6
In the Doghouse

It took ages to clean up. I knew I had to be quiet or I'd wake Mrs Harrison. But I kept dropping things.

When it was all done, I set the alarm for seven and fell into bed. I slept deeply. No dreams, not even of Grandad. I was woken by noisy rattling. I jumped out of bed. I grabbed the clock. Half past ten. I'd slept right through the alarm. So had Honey.

The rattling noise went on.

It was Mrs Harrison and Miss Pope. They were both calling to me through the letter box.

"Joe, Joe! Are you in there?"

I was still in my boxer shorts but at least the flat was spotless.

Miss Pope's visit went OK. I made her a cup of tea and served it to her on a tray, with sugar in a bowl. She was impressed by that.

Mostly we just chatted. She said she was worried I wasn't eating properly.

"I go shopping nearly every day," I said. "I need to. For Honey. I can't let her starve."

"For who?" said Miss Pope.

"My Grandad's dog."

Miss Pope smiled. "Oh, I see."

I said, "Grandad's really soft on her. But they won't let me take her into the hospital."

Miss Pope said, "Well, you do seem to be coping quite well for a boy of your age. I suppose I could let things stand as they are for another day or so. Shall I hold my report till next week?"

I was glad she didn't stay too long. I had to get ready to go to Grandad. On Saturdays, visiting started at midday. So I could spend almost the whole day with him.

As I was leaving, Mrs Harrison popped out of her flat.

"Here, take these to him," she said. She gave me a card and three oranges in a bag. "And give him all my very best wishes, won't you?"

"Yes, Mrs Harrison. Thank you."

"My, oh my! You were up late last night having a good time, weren't you? And you always look such a quiet lad."

So she *had* heard the noise.

"I'm ever so sorry if we kept you awake, Mrs Harrison. It wasn't my idea for them all to come round."

"No, dear. But then it never is, is it?"

Was she going to spill the beans?

She gave me a big wink. It was OK. I almost kissed her.

Chapter 7
Homework Time

The porter knew Honey well by now. And the nurses knew me. They were really kind, though they still couldn't let Honey in.

"Done your homework, Joe?" one of them asked.

"Nearly," I said.

I sat by Grandad's bed. He couldn't talk any more. I'm not even sure if he could see. But he could hear. I was sure of it. I held his hand so he'd know I was there.

I said, "Shall I read to you, Grandad?"

He didn't answer.

I read to him anyway. It was my essay for history homework about a boy getting his first job as a farm worker during the 1940s.

If Grandad could hear, he'd know it was all the stuff he'd told me about himself when he was young. Perhaps I'd made it sound a bit boring because he nodded off for a while. The nurse came over.

"Why don't you pop outside for a breath of fresh air, Joe?" she said. "Or go to the coffee shop?"

I went outside to see to Honey. The porter had already given her some water.

"Don't you worry about her," he said. "She's being as good as gold. I'll take her for a wee stroll during my break, if that's OK?"

"Thanks."

Grandad was still sleeping when I got back to the ward. So I sat by his bed and went through my Maths homework. The other men on the ward were having their tea brought round, so it was noisy in the ward. But by Grandad's bed we were quiet.

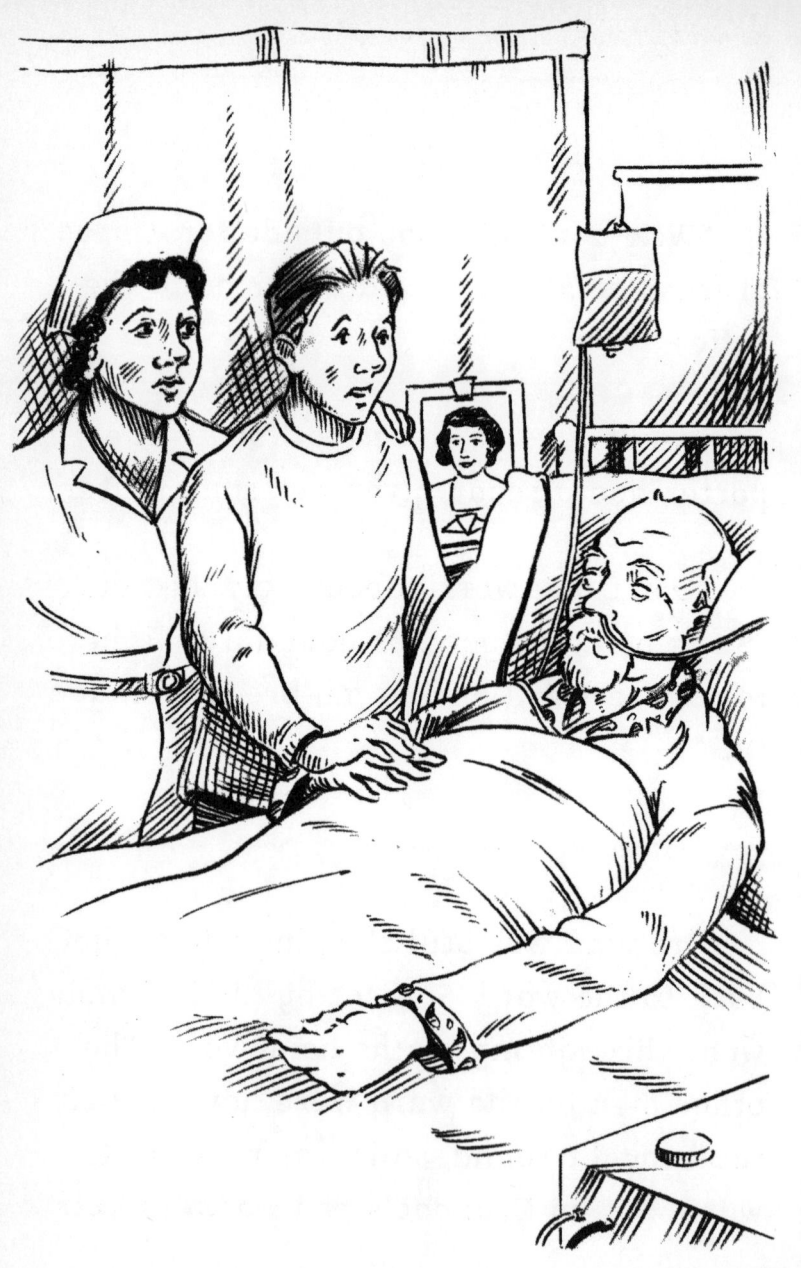

Then he died. Just like that. It wasn't scary. I didn't even realise at first.

The nurse came over. "He's gone, Joe," she said.

"No," I said. "He can't. Not yet. I'm not ready for him to go. He's just having a snooze."

She said, "He's really gone. There's nothing more we can do."

She was right. I had to let him go.

But I wanted to go on hanging on to him, holding his hand.

My Grandad, Joe.

I wanted to go on clinging on forever, just like he'd hung on to me when I was a kid.

I knew I was lucky. I'd been there when he died. I said, "I could have missed it so easily."

She nodded. She understood what I meant. I said, "And now there are things I have to do, aren't there? Getting the certificate from the doctor and all that legal stuff."

We'd had a talk at school from the Registrar of Births, Deaths and Marriages about being a responsible citizen.

The nurse said, "No, Joe. An adult will do that. I expect your social worker will see to it for you."

"But I'm his family." I felt I wanted to do whatever had to be done.

The nurse was saying something about what a wonderful old chap Grandad was and how much she'd liked looking after him. But I wasn't listening properly. My eyes had gone fuzzy.

She said, "Are you sure you're all right, Joe? Is there anyone you'd like to talk to?"

"It's OK. I'm fine." In a strange way I was. "But I've got to go and pick up Honey."

She smiled. "Yes. I'm glad you've got the dog. At least you won't have to explain anything to her. Dogs have a special way of understanding, don't they?"

I liked that nurse. She was good.

Chapter 8
Goodbye, Grandad

Miss Pope came running after me across the main entrance. On Saturday afternoons the hospital was always extra busy. It was more like a fun fair. The shop even had silver air balloons for sale. Visitors bought them for their sick friends and tied them to their beds to cheer them up. It made a change from flowers.

Miss Pope said, "Joe, I just wanted to tell you how very sorry I am about your grandfather."

"Thanks."

"If there's anything you feel you want to talk to me about – ?"

"Not really. These last weeks have been very important to me. I wouldn't have missed them for anything."

She looked at me oddly.

Quickly, I said, "I don't mean I enjoyed watching my Grandad being ill. I meant it's important that I've been here with him. I felt so close to him." I shouldn't even have tried to explain. "Excuse me, Miss Pope. But

I can't stop and chat now. I really have to be getting back home."

Suddenly, I wanted to be on my own so I could think about Grandad in my own way.

She said, "Joe, I'm not sure you fully understand what will happen next. Things are going to be very different for you from now on."

No need to tell me, I thought. "Yes. I know," I said.

"What I'm saying is, you won't be able to stay on in your grandfather's flat."

So what was going to happen to me and Honey?

She went on, "Someone will have to take care of you."

"Why?"

"It's the law. You're still under sixteen. You still count as a child. We'll sort out somewhere nice. Foster parents maybe. Or a hostel. I dare say you're looking forward to starting work as soon as you can so you can be independent? We can help you with that too. Just trust me." She gave me a weak smile.

"Grandad wants me to stay on at school." I said 'wants' as if he was still alive. "I mean, wanted. He wanted me to go to College. And there's Honey to think of too."

If Honey wasn't allowed into a hospital to visit her own master, I didn't suppose she'd be allowed to live in a hostel with me. But I don't think Miss Pope understood that Honey counted as part of my family.

"What about Honey?" I asked.

"She'll have to go into kennels for tonight. Then I'm sure we can find a good home for her. The RSPCA are always very helpful."

"She's already got a perfectly good home."

"Joe, listen to me. You cannot move back into the flat on your own. Now, you'll need to collect some overnight things. I'll drive you there."

I said, "The dog needs a walk." I needed a walk too.

"Oh very well. Promise me you'll be there. I'll come and pick you up at seven. That gives you two hours."

It didn't leave me much time to plan our future.

On the walk home I went through the choices. I could lock myself into the flat with Honey and see how long we could hold out. It wouldn't be long. Honey would get hungry.

I could run off with her and hope to find work somewhere. But what if there wasn't any? Honey would go hungry.

I could look for my Dad and see if he'd take us in. But what if he'd have me but wouldn't have Honey?

I said aloud, "They're all daft ideas, aren't they, Honey?" I knew I'd have to go along with whatever Miss Pope had in mind. Only one thing mattered. Making sure Honey was OK. I prepared what I'd say.

As soon as I got home, I wrote it down to make sure I wouldn't forget or be afraid to say it.

'Dear Miss Pope,' I wrote. 'I will do whatever you say is right, just so long as Honey and I can stay together.'

Then I decided to smarten both of us up for Miss Pope. I lifted Honey into the kitchen sink and bathed her. She didn't enjoy it.

"Sorry, but you have to suffer to be beautiful," I told her. I dried her with an old towel, then brushed her coat till it was smooth and glossy.

"That's you sorted," I said.

Then I got myself ready. I had a quick wash and put on clean clothes. I packed our things in a bag, Honey's rug and feeding dish, a couple of sweatshirts and Grandad's newspaper cuttings about the Battling Gran. Then I sat down as calmly as I could.

Honey knew something was up. She sat on the floor in front of me. I stroked her head gently. "There's my good girl. Not long now."

Her ears twitched. At seven o'clock on the dot we heard a car draw up, then footsteps on the path and a knock at the door. Miss Pope was on time. I stood up. Honey stood up and looked at me, her head on one side. It was almost as if she was asking, 'where are we going?'.

"I haven't a clue where we're going or what's to become of us. But as long as we stick together we'll be OK, won't we?"

She wagged her tail.

"Time to go, girl," I said. "Let's both be brave."

I took the lead and clipped it to her collar. I picked up our bag. We walked to the front door.

"Not to worry, girl," I whispered. "It's going to be all right."

I hope it is. It's got to be. Yes, it will be.

Honey looked up at me and wagged her tail.

I felt I could hear Grandad's voice saying, '*That's the way, lad. Go for it. Make something of your life*'.

Barrington Stoke would like to thank all its readers for commenting on the manuscript before publication and in particular:

Bernie Blayney
Hannah Boardman
James Bragg
Neil Coughlin
David Dutton
Lizzie Foote
Emma Fulford-Smith
Mark Jones
Fay Longdon
Anna Mackie
Bob Parker
Dorothy Porter
Paul Reilly
Dean Rigby

Become a Consultant!

Would you like to give us feedback on our titles before they are published? Contact us at the address or website below – we'd love to hear from you!

Barrington Stoke, 10 Belford Terrace, Edinburgh EH4 3DQ
Tel: 0131 315 4933 Fax: 0131 315 4934
E-mail:info@barringtonstoke.demon.co.uk
Website:www.barringtonstoke.co.uk

More Teen Titles!